STERLING and the distinctive Sterling logo are
registered trademarks of Sterling Publishing Co., Inc.

Library of Congress Cataloging-in-Publication Data

Norman, Kimberly.
Ten on the sled / by Kim Norman ; illustrated by Liza Woodruff.
p. cm.
Summary: Animals fall off a speeding sled one by one until only a lonely caribou is left,
chasing a giant snowball that has engulfed the falling animals.
ISBN 978-1-4027-7076-0 (hc-plc with jacket : alk. paper) [1. Stories in rhyme.
2. Sleds--Fiction. 3. Sledding--Fiction. 4. Animals--Fiction. 5. Counting.] I. Woodruff, Liza, ill. II. Title.
PZ8.3.N7498Te 2010
[E]--dc22   2009011501
Lot #:
2 4 6 8 10 9 7 5 3 1
04/10

Published by Sterling Publishing Co., Inc.
387 Park Avenue South, New York, NY 10016
Text copyright © 2010 by Kim Norman
Illustrations copyright © 2010 by Liza Woodruff
Distributed in Canada by Sterling Publishing
c/o Canadian Manda Group, 165 Dufferin Street
Toronto, Ontario, Canada M6K 3H6
Distributed in the United Kingdom by GMC Distribution Services
Castle Place, 166 High Street, Lewes, East Sussex, England BN7 1XU
Distributed in Australia by Capricorn Link (Australia) Pty. Ltd.
P.O. Box 704, Windsor, NSW 2756, Australia

Sterling ISBN 978-1-4027-7076-0

For information about custom editions, special sales,
premium and corporate purchases, please contact
Sterling Special Sales Department at 800-805-5489
or specialsales@sterlingpublishing.com.

Designed by Kate Moll
The illustrations were created using
watercolor, colored pencil, and pastel.

For Collin and Skylar,
my two on the sled.
—K.N.

For Thomas and Edie.
—L.W.

Ten
on the
Sled

by
Kim
Norman

illustrated by
Liza
Woodruff

STERLING

New York / London

On a sunlit night,
'neath a snowy moon,
there was ONE on the sled,
then TWO, but soon . . .

There were TEN on the sled
and the caribou said,
"Slip over! Slide over!"
So they all slid over,

and Seal spilled out.

There were NINE on the sled
and the caribou said,
"It's snowing! Get going!"
So they all got going,

but Hare

hopped

out.

There were EIGHT on the sled
and the caribou said,
"It's slicker! Go quicker!"
So they all went quicker,

but Sheep shot out.

There were SEVEN on the sled
and the caribou said,
"We're gliding! Keep riding!"
So they all kept riding,

but Walrus

whirled out.

There were SIX on the sled
and the caribou said,
"We're lighter! Hold tighter!"
So they all held tighter,

but Fox flipped out.

There were FIVE on the sled
and the caribou said,
"Great thunder! Duck under!"
So they all ducked under,

but Squirrel

Squeezed

out.

There were FOUR on the sled
and the caribou said,
"They're chasing! Keep racing!"
So they all kept racing,

but Wolf wiped out.

There were THREE on the sled
and the caribou said,
"They're winning! No spinning!"
So they all quit spinning,

but Moose

muddled out.

There were TWO on the sled
and the caribou said,
"Keep trying! We're flying!"
So they both kept flying,

till Bear bailed out.

There was ONE on the sled
and the caribou said,
"I'm only, I'm lonely,
I'm chilled to the bone.
A reindeer likes flying,
but never alone!"
So . . .

. . . ONE through TEN,
all leaped on again,
for one more run
and a little more fun
in the moonlit land
of the midnight sun.

THE END